Rise
and
Shine

Peter Marney

This book is dedicated to those who keep trying, no matter what.

Read this first

You are not a ninja.

It's very important that you know this fact.

It's very important because if you try to copy any of the stuff in this book then you might end up getting hurt or getting into trouble.

This will be bad.

This will be very bad because I'll get the blame.

So please, remember you're not a ninja and promise not to try and copy any of this stuff.

Have you promised?

Ok, you can now read on.

Trapped

There's a policeman's boot planted right next to my head and I think I've got a very good chance of going to prison for being stupid.

Stupid to think that things don't change and stupid for not noticing the new alarm system.

I'll explain everything in a moment but for now I'm trying not to sneeze while a trickle of sweat dribbles down my nose. My safety depends on staying absolutely still but my nose is beginning to tickle.

I can't move without being discovered and that mustn't happen.

In case you're wondering, I don't normally break into schools during the holidays and especially not my own school. It seemed like a good idea at the time but now I'm not so sure.

Normally I'd have Red and Keira to watch out for me but my stupidity extended to not telling them about this little trip. Well, they didn't want me to go shopping with them so I didn't want them here now.

Except that I do.

I wish they were here right now and I wish I'd never got into this mess.

It started last week when we were out shopping together.

"Jamie," says Keira, "Me and Red are going to look for some girly things. Can you amuse yourself for half an hour?"

Keira's my sort of Mum at the moment and Red's my best friend and a secret ninja just like me. I'll get onto that later.

I'm the original Red Sock Ninja except that it's Saturday and I wear yellow socks on a Saturday except when I'm trying to hide from policemen when I wear black socks and black jeans and a dark top.

That sweat drop is now dangling on the end of my nose and I'm desperately trying not to twitch.

There's nothing here Mr Policeman, so why not just shut the door, go back to your nice shiny police car, and drive off?

Why's he doing that?

Why's he decided to start moving boxes? What does he think he'll find?

Not me I hope!

His radio crackles.

"Mmmgff. Rrrung mmgff."

He moves to the doorway and steps into the corridor.

"375 to base. Repeat please, over."

"Over" means that he's finished and wants the other person to talk. I know this from reading my comics. Well, from listening to Red read my comics.

"Mmmgff, Anything to report, over."

They want to know what he's found. So do I, especially if it's about any cameras that might have my picture on them.

"Nothing here Sarge. Probably a faulty alarm. I'll have a word with the caretaker then get back to the station."

I breath a silent sigh of relief and, as soon as the door closes, wipe my nose. But that makes it tickle and twitch and I'm so not going to sneeze.

I'm not, I'm not, I'm…

"Ahhh…sssnff!"

A little ninja trick Keira taught me. If you breathe out just before you sneeze then it doesn't sound so noisy. Hopefully it worked and Mr Policeman isn't coming back to look for a mouse with a cold.

I freeze and wait for the door to reopen.

Nothing.

Safe at last.

Well, safe as in trapped in an alarmed building with possibly a caretaker still wandering about, but at least nobody's caught me yet. I'm also no closer to getting a library card.

Oh yes, I was explaining how I got here.

Well, while Keira and Red went off shopping without me, I popped into the town library. I'm not a member or anything but they've got better seats that most of the cafes and you don't have to buy a coffee.

I was pretending to look at some book while listening to my music when I realise this girl is looking at me. I don't get many girls doing that so I unplug my earphones.

"Not for boys," she whispers. "Silly girl's book. Words on book. Clue. About fairies."

"I was wondering if my sister might like it," I lie.

She just smiles and, takes the book out of my hand saying,

"Come, look here."

She talks a bit funny. It's English but a bit like Matt, my sort of friend who went back to Poland. Short simple words.

I follow her into this smaller room where she shows me a shelf of CDs.

"Don't need music," I say, pointing to the earphones dangling out of my pocket.

She looks a little like Naz, my other friend, but maybe a bit smaller.

"Not music, words."

She mimes opening a book.

"Book words."

Some lady wanders over to join us.

"I'm afraid you'll need a library card to borrow one of our audio books. Are you members?"

We both shake our heads and I think we're in trouble until she smiles.

"Never mind," she says. "I'll give you the forms and you can take them home."

Which is what I did and how Keira read that we need to prove who I am, which is kind of difficult because I'm not.

Well, obviously I am who I am. I'm just not who we say I am.

I'm supposed to be Jay, short for Jayden, but I'm really Jamie because we're in hiding. Me and the Red Sock Ninja Clan got into some trouble a while back and made enemies of some nasty people who might still be looking for us. That's why we had to run away and that's why I'm now called Jay.

It's also why I'm a bit lonely at the moment.

Things were ok when we were still at school but now everyone's gone home for the holidays we realise that we don't know anyone else.

Keira's got her brother Jack but me and Red have only got each other. We did have Naz but she's gone to stay with Dog Girl, one of her friends from school. Red could easily have gone as well but she didn't want to.

By the way, Dog Girl's really called Tamara but in my head she'll always be Dog Girl.

I'm only telling you this so you can understand why I got upset when the girls wanted to get rid of me and go shopping on their own.

It's been quiet for a while now so I suppose it's time to stop hiding and go home. I'll just stand up and stretch, carefully ease the door open and…

Peter Marney

Locked

Maybe it's just stiff.

Maybe if I shove the door handle down and really pull hard then this stupid door will spring open.

Or maybe someone's locked me in.

Nice.

Of course, all us secret ninjas have these special tools for opening locked doors so I just need to reach into my bag and grab my lock picks. That's just after I change my arm into a really long thin snake which can squeeze through the keyhole and slide all the way to my locker, which is where I stashed my bag after I broke in through the back window.

Last time this happened, at my old school, Red came and got me out. Like that's going to happen now and no, I don't do this all the time. Only some of the time and we don't usually get caught.

It was Red who taught me how to open locks without using the proper key and Keira who gave me my lock picks as a Christmas present. Yes, I know that's a bit weird but you haven't met Keira yet.

Anyway, Red's first lesson involved a paper clip rather than a proper lock pick, so I suppose it's sort of handy that I just happen to be sitting in our Supply Cupboard.

I'm in the cupboard because Miss Rainey's printer has run out of ink and I was in her office because I needed her computer because I needed to forge a letter from her saying I'm who we say I am, so I can join the library, so I can get an audio book because I can't read.

There, I've said it!

I can't read. I'm ten and a half years old and I read like an infant.

It's not my fault. My old teacher said I've got this disease or something which scrambles my brain when I try to read letters. I'm not thick or anything. It's just that my brain is wired up a bit different.

Anyway, I've found the paperclips and got one of the big ones into this lock. It's better if I close my eyes to do this bit.

Click!

Being a secret ninja isn't all about fighting and climbing buildings.

Sometimes it's about details.

Tiny details like putting everything back exactly as it was so that nobody knows you've been opening desk drawers to steal passwords and opening a box of paper clips to escape.

I've got to work quickly, collect my bag and get out of here before I set off another alarm. Two alarms in one day and Mr Policeman will be back with friends to do a proper search.

I've also got to break back into our flat through my bedroom window before Keira finds out I've gone missing. I'm supposed to be sulking in my room.

Did you know that you can make an alarm system out of some empty drinks cans, a drawing pin and a piece of string or cotton?

No, I didn't either, which is why I'm halfway through our window when the cans crash to the floor and the light comes on.

Now, do I tell the truth or make up a story?

I've just tried the truth and I don't think Keira's happy.

"Jamie, of all the stupid things you've ever done, this is the stupidest. It's beyond stupid. It's so stupid that the King of Planet Stupid would make you Professor Stupid of Stupid University for that level of stupidity."

I told you she wasn't happy.

Red's sensibly gone to hide in her bedroom and I think I want to join her. Maybe it wasn't a good idea to tell Keira I nearly got caught as well.

"What made you think it's ok to break into school?"

Well, we've sort of done it before, remember, when you put that smelly stuff in Dog Girl's slippers. No, perhaps it's best not to remind her about that just now. Better to stay quiet and let her rant.

Which she does.

For another ten minutes.

Then I have to explain exactly why I was doing such a stupid thing which is why Keira is now showing both of us how to do it properly.

This time we pick the lock on Miss Rainey's window and climb straight into her office. We don't need the printer because Keira has a data stick to copy the letter we forge on the computer.

Then we put everything back as we found it and go home to print the letter on Keira's printer using the paper we stole from the desk. Miss Rainey won't even notice the two missing sheets or the envelope.

It's probably not a good idea to show Keira how good I am at forging signatures so I let her write Miss Rainey's name on the bottom of the letter which I'm now showing the lady at the library.

Which is why I'm now being punched.

I could fight back and I'd probably win, even though he's bigger than me, but I don't want to upset Amy.

Amy's my friend from the library who's still learning English because she's from somewhere called Iraq which is a long way away. She showed me on a map.

We'd been meeting in the library twice a week, whispering to each other because libraries are supposed to be quiet places. She's also helping me with reading because "it important to learn English so you fit in".

She's staying with an uncle because her parents are still in Iraq she thinks. Somehow she forgot to mention her brother but that's ok because he's the one introducing himself with his fists.

For some reason he doesn't like me.

If I could speak their language maybe I'd work out what they're yelling at each other but even without words I can tell that me and him aren't going to be friends any time soon.

I can't see the problem. All I was doing was walking along the street with Amy, laughing about some silly joke or something.

I can dodge most of his punches but a few are landing and they hurt.

Amy's been yelling "Brother. Don't hurt", which I guess is aimed at me, so I've only hitting back with a few light jabs to try and put him off which is so not happening.

I'm using all of my boxing skills to keep dodging his punches but he just keeps hitting me.

That's when I hear Red.

"Jay, stop messing around and thump him!"

Distracted, I miss an incoming hook which connects to my eye and throws me to the floor.

Big mistake.

Before I can get up, Red flies in with a kick to his leg and another to his guts, landing him on his bottom.

I'm up and grabbing Red before she can do more damage. I've seen her fight like this before and it can get messy.

Hearing the sound of a siren, which is never good news, I grab her and we both run off before we have to start answering difficult questions from angry policemen.

I wonder if Amy still likes me?

Peter Marney

Fighting

I'm in trouble again but this time it's worse.

This time it's double trouble.

Keira's mad at me for getting into a fight and Red's mad at me because…

Actually, I've no idea why Red's mad at me but she is. She's gone all sulky and keeps the door of her bedroom shut.

"Why d'you get into a fight then Jamie?"

I only sort of lie.

"Don't know."

It's true, I don't know why he started hitting me.

"Well, it's back to the gym for you Mr Stupid."

That's her new name for me by the way.

"If someone can bruise your eye like that, then you need some more boxing practice!"

And that's why I'm now dripping with sweat and ready to drop.

For the past week, Keira's had me down the gym and working out every single day. Running, skipping, thumping punching bags and getting thumped by her every time I let my concentration slip.

We're back on the mat, fighting again, and I could get a few shots back at her but I reckon I'm in enough trouble as it is.

"Jamie, you're fighting like a wet blondie!"

That's my favourite term for some of the girls at school.

"I've given you three chances to punch me and you've missed every one of them. Either fight to win or stop wasting my time!"

That remark comes with a left handed slap which I nearly dodge.

"You've got three minutes to put me on the floor before I tear up your library card!"

I charge at her, fists flying, but she easily dodges out of the way.

"Stop flapping like a blondie. Fight like a ninja!"

She's right!

I've got my brain in a muddle and I'm fighting like a five year old.

It's not a proper fight and Keira's not trying to rip my head off. If she was then by now you'd have heard a soggy squelch as it bounced on the floor.

She could beat me just using her kicks if she wanted to, so this is all about me. About if I can still fight.

I take a deep breath and relax. Tense muscles are slow muscles Keira says.

She's dropped her right hand so I aim a kick to her head except that I'm only pretending. Keira never drops her guard so it's got to be a trap.

She moves to block the kick which I've pulled out of and leaves her left side open to the punch which I land before quickly pulling away.

I can see that one hurt but I've got to keep going. She's trying to grab my arm and turn this into a judo match but I spin into her body and plant an elbow in her ribs before spinning away again.

That's slowed her up a bit.

Watch the eyes, always watch the eyes Keira says.

I can see her glance over my shoulder but that's another trick I'm not falling for.

I pretend to look but instead aim a kick at her head which I know she's going to block. Well, she would block it if my leg was there, which it isn't. Instead I've planted it on the floor and used my other leg to sweep around and jab her knee just enough for it to collapse and take her body to the floor.

This is where I step in for the kill.

Except that I don't.

Instead I step back and, putting my hands together, I bow deeply towards her.

Keira is my teacher, my Sensei. She's also my friend who's now bowing back to me.

"Well done Jamie."

Then somehow she's hugging me and it's all good again.

I even get a chocolate milkshake.

"Now Jamie, what have you done to upset Red?"

We're whispering across the cafe table so she's using my real name.

I shrug.

"Don't know."

She gives me one of her looks.

"No, I really don't know. I know she's upset about something and I guessed it was my fault somehow but I haven't got a clue. I know she's missing her Mum but it's more than that."

We agree it's a mystery and that Keira will try and chat to Red to find out what's wrong.

The other good thing is that I'm now allowed back to the library. Amy's not here but it's only a matter of time. She loves books too much to stay away.

But she does.

The ladies in the library know me by sight and they all smile at me.

"I'm usually trying to get kids into the library but you need to get out Jay. Go spend some time with your friends in the sunshine."

I would do, if my friend was still talking to me.

"Here," she says, handing me a leaflet, "have a look at this. Might be fun."

I pretend to read it and smile, thanking her as I tuck it into my pocket. Maybe Keira will read it to me later or I'll try and sound out the words. There's a picture of some smiling kids but I can't figure out what they're doing.

After a while I wander home and walk straight into a job.

"Washing day Jamie," says Keira cuddling a bundle of dirty clothes. "You've been wearing those jeans for ages. Go change and bring out all your stuff."

I give my jeans a sniff as I take them off. Smell all right to me. Now the socks under my bed, those are a different story!

I bundle everything up and take it to Keira then scuttle away to hide before she gives me something nasty to do.

"Jamie!"

Now what have I done?

"What happens when you put paper in the washing machine?"

I didn't do it deliberately and anyway, perhaps those things needed a second wash last week.

"Did you empty your pockets?"

Oops.

"If so, then what's this?"

Ah, the thing from the library. I'd forgotten about that.

"Last week it was a shopping list and the week before that your pocket money. Don't you ever learn?"

Apparently not.

Well, I do learn but I also tend to forget stuff sometimes, especially when I'm daydreaming which I'm probably doing a lot lately.

Oh no!

Keira's smiling. That's never good news.

"This should get you out from under my feet."

She's waving that leaflet in the air.

Peter Marney

A whole new world

Dirty, dark, dismal, and any other words I can think of beginning with "D".

Dreadful, that's another good one. I am full of dread looking at the building in front of us.

Keira double checks the address on the leaflet but we seem to be in the right place. So where have all the smiling kids disappeared to then?

It's a low long building which someone forgot to knock down when they built the surrounding estate. It's well old and dingy, another good "D" word.

It might help if the sun was shining but the overcast drizzle just seems to complete the picture of desolation. Ok, I'm exaggerating but I wanted to get in one last "D" word.

Red gives the door a shove and it reluctantly lets us into a sort of mini hall all painted black. Muffled music is coming from behind one of the doors so we continue to investigate.

Have you ever seem one of those cowboy films where, as the good guy walks into the saloon, the piano stops and everyone turns to stare at him?

I reach for my six shooter but I'm in the wrong film. Out of the corner of my eye I can see Red lift her hands out of her pocket. No reason for it to get nasty but no reason not to be prepared either.

"What are you two doing here?"

We turn towards a somehow familiar voice.

"No, I didn't mean it like that. It's lovely to see you but shouldn't you have gone home for the holidays?"

It's Miss G, the new dance teacher from school. What's she doing here?

"It's all a bit political back home at the moment," lies Keira. "So we decided to stay. Got room for two more?"

Room in what?

No, Keira hasn't told me what the leaflet's about and she hid it from Red to make this all a big surprise.

"You joking? Of course we've got room for more. I can always use a trained dancer and a tekky."

Me, a trained dancer?

"Come on in and I'll bring you up to speed."

Everyone else gets five minutes to relax while someone at last tells us what's going on.

"The show's on Monday night but you didn't miss much last night. Mainly team building and deciding on parts."

Hold on a minute. Show?

What show?

Monday night?

This Monday night?

No, she can't mean this Monday night. It's Saturday today. Why is she still smiling? It's impossible! It took us weeks to put our end of term school dance piece together and it was a shambles. No way can she do a show in three days.

"Cat, I'd like you to help me with the dancers and Jay, the tekky hole's up that ladder. Go have a play and we'll talk later about lighting. No chance you can stay as well is there?"

This last question is aimed at Keira who's already halfway out of the door and shaking her head. So we're being abandoned then.

"Pick you up at six," she says before running away.

Thanks Keira.

Thanks for dumping me in this dirty, dusty hole with one skylight view of the real world and a letterbox cut out of the wall so I can see a stage space. No stage though, just a room with a few groups of kids sitting round reading.

At least I can work out what the pile of junk on the table is supposed to be. Lighting desk, sound, a CD player and an amplifier. All a busy tech boy needs to run a show.

A head appears at the top of the ladder.

Why is Miss G always smiling?

"Yes, I know it's old and horrible but it's all we've got and only because people give us stuff rather than throw it away. Welcome to a show on a shoestring. No stage, no set, no proper actors and no money. You'll love it!"

Maybe I will when I work out what a shoestring is. Oh, and what she means by set. A jelly sets in the fridge when it goes from liquid to a wobbly solid. Perhaps the show's going to be a bit wobbly.

"Cat's learning some dance moves with the girls so I've got five minutes. Let me give you the tour."

It doesn't take that long.

Toilets, changing room, junk room, and what Miss describes as the theatre. Really it's a load of seats at one end and a lighting rig at the other. I say rig but it's just a couple of lamps hanging off the wall each side and a few more on a ceiling bar.

"We're borrowing a few more lights tonight and Trev's rigging them up for us. You know Trev."

Do I?

I do.

I recognise him when he turns up later. It's Mr Tekky who set up the lamps for our school show. Except this time it's me up the ladder while he tells me what to do.

Rigging means setting everything up so it's safe and won't hurt anyone. Anything hung from the bar has a double chain so it can't drop on an actor and all leads are taped to the floor so nobody trips over them.

"If it's possible to trip over anything, an actor will find it," Trev says.

I don't think he likes actors.

"And a dancer'll fall over it even after it's taped solid."

He hates dancers even more than actors.

Welcome to the wonderful world of working backstage.

Actually, it's really interesting and I get to do loads of cool stuff. Trev double checks everything and sorts out my mistakes. Well, he shows me how to sort out my own mistakes and tells me why it needs to be his way and not my way.

I learn more today that in a whole term at school.

I get to see the other kids on breaks but they're mostly still practising their dance moves or learning the songs. Red seems happy enough but I notice doesn't make an effort to come and join me.

Guess she's still mad at me for something.

Wish I knew what.

Then the door opens and my day
goes from good to great to horrible
in a matter of seconds.

Peter Marney

Girlfriends

Guess who just walked through the door?

She's wearing one of those funny scarf things but I still recognise Amy and start to grin until I see who's following her.

She spots me straight away but doesn't come and say hello, just smiles a bit from a distance. This is going to be awkward.

Big brother's not so shy and comes over to stand in front of me. Suddenly Red notices what's happening, decides to be my friend after all, and strides across to stand next to me. If there's going to be another fight, then we're ready.

"Malik! There you are. I was hoping you'd turn up."

At least Miss G seems pleased by our new arrivals.

"Jay, this is Malik and over there's Amira, his sister. They're from Iraq and staying here for a while, aren't you Ami."

Ami?

"Malik's our builder. He's a whizz with tools and can make anything."

You let him near sharp things? This is getting better by the minute.

"Ami's the singer of the family. Girls, take Ami through the songs while I sort out the set with

Malik. Cat dear, could you rehearse the dancers in that last number again please?"

She means Red. Red's called Cat for the same reason that I'm called Jay. Yes, I know it's confusing but that's the life of a secret ninja sometimes.

So now there's just the three of us stood here.

I wonder if I should say something to Miss G.

"I go make set," Malik says as he walks away.

Yes, go make set. Go make anything. Go make yourself disappear and don't come back.

I scurry back up my ladder before Miss decides Malik needs an assistant and I turn it sideways. If anyone else wants to use it then I'll hear them coming.

Of course, nothing happens so I get busy tidying up leads and stuff. I like my tech tidy because then I can see where everything goes and where it comes from. The lamps all come through this cable which splits out into the desk with these wires. The speakers go to that desk and this loose wire goes…

I don't know where it goes because I don't know where it comes from or what it does. That's why I'm stretched out on the floor following the wire down to a hole when a foot appears pressing against my neck and pinning me to the ground.

That thudding noise is my heart by the way and it's suddenly difficult to swallow. How'd he get up that ladder so quietly?

The foot lifts but, as I raise my head, something crashes into my ribs.

"That's for being stupid!"

Red?

"Ouch, that hurts!"

"Good."

Just what I need, another fight.

"What's the point in moving the ladder if you don't listen for it? And what's your girlfriend doing here?"

My what?

"No, she's just someone I met in the library. I…"

"Don't lie Jamie, I've seen the way she looks at you!"

I haven't.

At least if I have I don't know what it's supposed to mean.

"Honest Red, she's not. How am I supposed to know what she thinks? You know I can't read people."

That gets me a shove.

"Dummy!"

Well, it's better than being kicked.

"So that's what the fight was about. Big brother doesn't want you messing around with his little sister."

What?

How'd she work that out? Malik didn't say anything and Amy didn't seem bothered about talking to me in the library. I hate this sort of stuff. It gets me all confused when nobody says what they mean.

"So she's not your girlfriend?"

I shake my head.

"Then who are you going to tell first?"

About what? I'm still confused.

It's a good job Red knows me so well. She can see the look on my face and sits down to explain everything.

"Ami needs to know that she's just a friend and the big guy needs to know that you don't fancy his sister. Which one you going to tell first?"

Easy, I tell Amy or Ami or whatever she's called.

"Wrong!"

Why wrong? If I tell her then she can sort out her brother. Easy.

"Wrong! You tell Ami, she bursts into tears and goes running to big bro who comes looking for you for another fight for making his sister cry."

Ok, then I tell him first.

"Wrong!"

This is a stupid game.

"You tell him, and he tells her. She hates you for not telling her first, bursts into tears and he comes looking for that fight again."

Why is everything so complicated? I reckon the best answer is to forget the whole thing and run off home.

"Not interrupting anything am I?"

Miss G's head pops up the ladder followed by the rest of her.

"Only we need to talk about lighting Jay."

"No problem Miss, just finding out if Jay's ok. Haven't seen him much today. I'll get back to the dancers shall I?"

Red doesn't wait for an answer and slides down the ladder.

"Well, you kept that quiet Jay. Didn't realise Cat's your girlfriend."

Neither did I. How many girlfriends have I got?

Miss tells me the sort of lighting she wants for the show and I play about with the switches while she looks at the stage.

She's not happy.

"Every year it's the same. Too much to do and not enough time. I can't do a lighting plot and run the rehearsals and look after all these kids. I need to keep an eye on Malik as well. He doesn't seem very happy at the moment."

I wonder why.

That's when I have my idea and that's why I now get to hide in my box and no one is allowed to disturb me.

Like the rest of my life, I'm going to make up the lighting for the show as it happens. Miss isn't convinced but, as I did such a great job with the school show, she's willing to trust me.

Naz is the real expert with the lighting but she's gone off on holiday. Got herself invited to spend time with Dog Girl and her Mum at their big house and go riding every day and play tennis and go shopping and I got bored by then but there could be more fun stuff to do at Dog Mansions if I'd bothered to keep listening.

What I can't work out is why Red didn't go as well. She got invited and Naz is her best friend so it doesn't make sense.

Anyway, without Naz to help me with the lighting I've got to sort of imagine what I want to happen and then see if I can move the sliders and switches to create the picture on stage. It sounds daft but I can sort of see it in my head rather than explain it. That's why I need the thinking time.

I also need to think about how to sort out Malik before he tries to sort me out with his fists again.

What do you reckon I should do?

Illegal

You remember that bit where I get to hide in my tech hole?

Well, forget it.

Apparently there's been some arguments and name calling and general bitchiness and Miss has called us all together.

"I'm disappointed in you!"

She looks angry.

"All of you!"

Definitely angry.

"Most of you know how this works and you should be teaching those who don't. We either all work together or the whole thing sinks. Everyone's equal and we need all of you."

That's good to know.

"But if all you can do is mess around and argue then the door's over there and you can close it behind you on the way out!"

Something's really upset her.

"It's been a long day and as usual we're well behind but I've had enough. Go home, learn the songs, work on the dance steps, and decide if you really want to be a part of this."

She suddenly looks exhausted.

"Nine o'clock start tomorrow. If you're late then don't be surprised if I kick you out. Go!"

Everyone's looking down at the floor and avoiding eye contact. They just want to get out of here and quickly grab their coats and shoes and stuff before scurrying out of the door.

"Cat, Jay, wait behind please."

Now what have we done?

"Sorry about that," Miss says, "but it needed saying. Doesn't apply to you two though. I need both of you."

That's good to hear.

"Actually, I need more than both of you. Some friends I was expecting to turn up and help have let me down and I can't manage on my own. I need to be everywhere and it isn't happening."

Well, I'd love to clone myself and have lots of me running around but that's not going to happen is it, so what can we do?

"Any chance you can persuade Keira to stay tomorrow?"

Which is why I'm now being shouted at by my babysitter for the second time.

"No, no, and no! And stop whinging Jamie, I'm not doing it!"

That was the first time and before Red chatted to her after I'd stormed out of the room and slammed the door.

Ok, I shouldn't have slammed it quite so hard but I was angry. Anyway, it gave Red a chance to try a different approach which must have worked.

"Jay, if you don't sort out your left from your right in the next ten seconds you can give me ten press ups!"

That's the second bit of shouting and explains why I'm on the floor even if it's not really my fault.

Red was so keen to get here early that we rushed out and I forgot my watch. It goes on my left wrist and reminds me which is my left side.

Without it, I'm getting confused, especially as Keira is making all of us run about like mad ferrets during her warm up.

"You!" She's pointing at Malik. "If you think that's funny, you can do the same. Ten press ups!"

Ami translates and Malik hits the floor.

Actually the translation lasted a bit longer that I think it should and she must have been persuading him to do as Keira said or else.

As I finish my punishment and jump up I spot a couple of guys walking through the door.

They look like trouble.

Keira must have seen the look on my face because she's already on her way over to them and her hands are nice and loose by her side. She's ready to fight if necessary.

Just as she's about to get into trouble, Jack walks in behind them and grins at his sister.

"Thought they'd knocked this place down years ago," he says by way of introduction.

"This is Baz and Tufty. What needs doing?"

Keira gives him a hug and points him towards Miss G before getting us all on the floor for more press ups.

I miss the next bit because my nose is pointing downwards but Miss G then splits us into teams for some more games where we have to carry each other and work together. By then, Jack and his mates have disappeared into another room.

These new games might be fun if I didn't have Malik in my team. Somehow he just manages to bump me whenever we're close or get in the way or generally make a nuisance of himself.

I'm not the only one to notice.

"Malik, come to me please," says Miss and they disappear into the other room. The rest of us carry on under the shouting of Keira until they come back when Miss decides to finish the torture and get us to work properly.

At least I now know the names of a few more kids.

Most of my work is done for the moment until I can see the show on stage and decide how to light it. With time to spare I go walkabout to find out what the rest are up to.

Jack's mates are builders and they're messing about with wood and saws, building our set, which I learn means the scenery and stuff on stage which make it look like where we're pretending it is. Jack's gone off to "beg, borrow or steal" a few things we're still missing and Keira's just sort of wandering around and helping out wherever needed.

Miss pulls me to one side.

"Sorry about Malik," she says.

I just smile. What else can I do?

"They're going through a rough time at the moment. The authorities want to send them back to Iraq."

I didn't know they could do that sort of thing but they can because Amy and Malik aren't supposed to be here. They're illegal immigrants.

"I can't imagine the pressure of having to hide every day in case you get found out. The threat of being put in jail again."

I can.

Again? Did she just say again? They've already been in jail?

"Anyway, that's why he might seem a bit unfriendly at the moment."

I tell Miss it's not a problem and I'll try to stay out of his way, which I was going to do anyway, and she thanks me for being so kind.

I'd sort of forgotten that the Red Sock Ninjas are still being hunted as well but Miss's little chat has reminded me.

Thanks for that, Miss.

Now I'm going to be looking over my shoulder every time I walk home for the next few weeks.

Peter Marney

Hijab

Red's having an argument with Amy which isn't good for me.

Who do I support?

"Don't be daft. How can a piece of cloth make a difference? It's just because you're new. We had the same when we first got here."

Amy's been saying that she gets treated differently now she's wearing her scarf which she calls a hijab. Red thinks that's rubbish and I agree, though I decide not to get involved because I just know it'll only end up with both girls shouting at me.

Luckily Miss calls an end to the break and everyone's crowded into the stage room so we can run through the show for the first time. I escape up my ladder and watch through the hole in the wall.

It isn't pleasant.

When you see a proper show on stage, everything runs smoothly and it looks so easy.

This doesn't.

It stops and starts and stutters and everyone's on edge. Miss yells at people to move where they're supposed to be and yells at everyone to sing louder but it's still a shambles.

"Stop!" Miss shouts from the piano.

Everybody freezes and I put all the lights on.

"It's rubbish. It's always rubbish and you know it. First run throughs always go wrong so stop worrying about getting it perfect and just do the best you can. Now from the start of that last number."

And so we carry on until the bitter end.

"Ten minutes break and then notes."

She disappears from sight and her head pops up through my floor.

"Remind you of anything Jay?"

Our class number for the school show was just as bad.

"It always crashes like that so don't get worried. Gives you an idea of the show though so you can do something with the lights?"

She sounds more hopeful than I'd like. Good lighting isn't going to rescue this disaster.

I nod and grin so as not to upset her and she disappears to talk to the rest of them while I sit and think about lights.

I'm busy daydreaming when Amy pops her head up the ladder, except it's not Amy.

"Red, why are you wearing that silly scarf. Amy convinced you to join her lot?"

Apparently it's a bet which is why we're both now walking down to the shops and why we're getting some really funny looks.

First it's the glance at the hijab and then it's a proper stare when they see that Red is white.

Red's just acting her normal self but even the lady in the shop seems a bit odd when we go to pay for our cans of drink. She doesn't say anything about the scarf but doesn't chat either like people normally do.

Maybe that bit of cloth does make a difference after all. Wonder what would happen if I wore it.

When we get back there's another surprise for us.

Naz and Dog Girl are standing there with Keira and looking a bit shocked.

Seems that Keira wanted to surprise all of us by not telling me and Red they were coming and not telling them what they were walking into.

It's hugs all round and I even get one from Dog Girl which is a first. She must have been really desperate to get away from her mother to be pleased enough to give me a hug. We haven't exactly been friends.

I let the girls gossip and get introduced to everyone else while I disappear up my ladder.

"More friends?"

It seems I have an unwelcome guest.

"Yes Malik, more friends. From my school."

I revert to simple words like I used to use with Matt, my Polish friend.

"Cat your girlfriend?"

That's not an easy question to answer so I decide to lie a little bit.

"Yes Malik, Cat's my girlfriend."

He smiles for the first time.

"Not Ami?"

"No Malik, Amy's just a friend from library. Not girlfriend."

I'm not sure how much English he really understands but I think he's got the idea.

He makes his way to the ladder.

"Good," he says as he disappears.

Now all I need to do is tell Amy before he does which proves a lot easier than I imagined.

"Amy, there's something I want to tell you," I start.

"I know. We just library friends, yes?"

Well, yes but how did she know?

"Cat told me. She my friend also now. Like Natalia and Tammy."

Girls sure make friends quickly.

"It was funny," Red told me later. "Ami took one look at Naz and started rattling away in Iraqi or whatever she speaks. Poor Naz just stood there blank."

I know the feeling. I have that trouble with English most days.

"Anyway, once we'd sorted that out, she just sort of started chatting to us between the songs and dances. I think she's happy she won the bet."

It's true. People do treat you differently if you're wearing one of those things. Odd isn't it?

"She's not bad for a singer but dances a bit like you."

Poor girl.

Red prattles on happily but I'm only half listening. Why should a bit of cloth make such a difference? I mean, it's only clothes. Dancers wear all sorts of odd things but nobody treats them differently. I suppose in Iraq, we'd be the ones being stared at because we're not wearing the same as everyone else.

Ouch!

Red's just hit me in the ribs again.

"I said, do you agree?"

I nod rather than risk more bruising which is why our flat is now full of giggling girls. Apparently I agreed to a sleep over and Keira didn't mind as I was happy with the idea.

Have I told you how crafty Red can be sometimes?

I decide to sneak out for a run but get caught putting on my trainers.

"Can I come?"

Possibly the last three words I ever expected to hear from Dog Girl.

"Miss G says I've got to build up my stamina and anyway, I need to give my ears a rest for five minutes."

It is getting noisy out there.

Keira tells me to look after Tammy and then we're off. I keep it down to a gentle jog but that only allows her to start chatting.

"Nat says your Dad's left home too."

Just how much has Naz told her I wonder? I'll have to be careful. We're supposed to be in hiding and the last thing we want is someone else knowing all about us.

"Why do they do that?" she asks.

And that's the question I've been trying to ignore for the past couple of years. Why did Dad have to leave like that?

I blink away the tears forming in my eyes. Must be the wind getting into them because it's happening to Dog Girl as well. I stop to give mine a wipe and suddenly I'm surrounded by sobbing girl.

Luckily Red's told me what to do in these situations so I put my arms around her and let her just cry until she's finished.

But what do I do next?

Race

In the next ten minutes I learn more about Dog Girl than I ever wanted to, but at least she's stopped crying. I manage to get her jogging again with the excuse that I'm getting cold.

I also get an apology.

"I've been very mean to you Jay and I'm sorry."

I glance across at her but she's looking firmly forward.

We've been very mean to her as well but I hope that Naz didn't mention the thing with the ballet shoes. I can still remember the smell.

"Forgive me?"

No! You were mean and horrible and I didn't deserve it. But I'm not stupid enough to say that out loud. Red's taught me that much.

"Please?"

I hate it when girls just keep on at you.

"Only if you can beat me home!"

I speed up but let her win the race to our front door. No point in having another sulky girl about the flat. I'd had enough of that from Red, who's now giving me another strange look as we come back into the living room.

"Tell you later," I whisper on the way past to the shower.

At least I can get some privacy there.

Which is more than I can say for the rest of the night with snoring bodies everywhere once they'd finally put down their scripts and finished singing the songs from the show.

Breakfast isn't much better but at least it's over quickly as we're on an early start.

For once, I'm glad to be inside for the day as the weather's horrible. Big black clouds and the trees going mad as the wind tries to blow their branches off.

"No chance of a run today then Jay," says Dog Girl smiling at me.

I decide I like this weather.

The hut's already busy when we get there and Jack's mates must have been working half the night because we now have a proper stage and some scenery.

Everyone looks tired but we soon liven up after some warm up exercises and some running games. I notice that Amy and her brother haven't arrived yet and there are another couple of latecomers with excuses about silent alarm clocks and cars which wouldn't start.

It's less than twelve hours to go before the proper show but everyone seems much more relaxed than yesterday. Hardly anything goes wobbly and it's actually sounding musical.

Something's wrong.

Amy's just walked in and I can tell by the look on her face that something is definitely wrong. She goes over to whisper to Miss and gets a hug in return which isn't good news by the look on Miss G's face.

I miss what happens next because Tufty calls to me wanting help to move some stuff.

"How difficult would it be to move those cables?"

That's easy.

All you have to do is unscrew all of the wires from the lighting box and the sound box. The impossible bit is putting them all back in again. That's probably going to take all day because nothing ever goes back how it was without something breaking or going all wobbly somehow.

"If it's not broken then don't fix it," I tell him.

It's something my Dad used to say to me, usually after I'd got all the bits of the video player or something spread across the kitchen table. How else was I going to find out how it worked?

Tufty nods.

"Fair comment. Only I'd be happier if this cable didn't go across the floor like that. Never mind."

Then he's off to do another job and I'm left to play with the lights before Miss restarts the show on stage.

It's a bit hard to hear what Miss is saying from up here because of the noise of the wind. We could really do with headsets but instead she gets Naz to stand at the bottom of the ladder and shout instructions up to me.

Because Naz and Dog Girl came late, they're only in a couple of numbers and Miss has been using them as dance teachers and assistants and general run arounds. It's a good job Miss doesn't know just how good Naz is with lighting or I'd be the one at the bottom of the ladder.

We're half way through the number when there's this huge crash from behind the stage.

"Stop!" shouts Miss, closely following with "What was that?"

Jack and Tufty go running backstage to investigate and Miss gets everyone else off of the stage and up to the other end of the room.

"Nothing here," comes a shout. "Must be up in the loft. Jay, can you bring your ladder over here please."

I scramble down as Tufty comes to help me carry it.

Jack dashes outside to look at the roof and is quickly back.

"It's not a problem and we can fix it."

That doesn't sound like good news.

"It's just a tree branch sticking out of the roof."

Miss looks worried.

"All we need to do is get up there, get rid of it and patch up the hole. Stick a taup over it or something."

Red's appeared beside me and is whispering in my ear.

"Tarpaulin. It's a waterproof cover. Like you see on some lorries."

Thanks for that Red.

"Oh, and I think Dog Girl fancies you."

What?!!!

I turn to ask a thousand questions but Red's already walking away and grinning at me. At least someone thinks it's funny.

Tufty and Jack stick the ladder by the trapdoor to the roof space and Jack grabs a torch before climbing to the top while me and Tufty hold the ladder steady. As he opens the trap I see daylight in the roof space which means it's probably a big hole.

Jack starts to shine his torch about but then ducks down and slams the trap back over the space before sliding quickly downwards.

"Everybody out now!" he shouts. "Grab your stuff and get out. Grab everything because you're not coming back!"

Peter Marney

Asbestos

Asbestos.

It's what builders used to line the inside of roofs until scientists found out that it can kill you. It's alright in big lumps and if it's not disturbed but if it breaks up, the small fibres can get into your lungs and do serious damage.

Why is Jack telling us this?

Well, guess what's up in that roof space and what's just been all broken up by a tree branch crashing down on it?

"But if we seal the trapdoor, can't we just do the show tonight and then get out?" Miss asks hopefully.

"One, we don't know how much damage is up there. Two, if it's weakened the floor and the rain gets in, then that could go as well. And three, it's just too dangerous to let kids in with those fibres about."

I think that means no. No, we can't just do the show.

Miss gathers everybody together in the car park and tells us that it's all over. No show, and probably the end of the project forever.

"We needed to sell tickets to get us the money we need for next year. That's how it works. No money, no project."

"We find other stage?"

I didn't notice Malik turn up but he's just asked the question.

"No Malik, they knocked the theatre down years back to build a shopping centre," Miss explains. "No other stage."

I put up my hand.

"Jay, you're not in school, you don't have to put your hand up."

"No Miss, I know I'm not in school but the stage is and lights and sound."

She runs over and gives me a big hug while I go bright red with embarrassment.

"Of course we've got a stage! Jay, you're brilliant!"

She grabs her mobile and calls Miss Rainey. She explains what's happened, which takes a few minutes, but the answer comes straight back.

"But…"

Miss listens some more and then hangs up.

"She say no?"

You really need to ask that Malik? Can't you see the look on Miss G's face.

It starts to rain.

"Everybody back to our flat."

Has Keira gone mad? How we going to put our show on there?

I'm close enough to hear her next whisper.

"Jack, I need an untraceable phone in the next ten minutes. Know where to get one?"

He nods and runs off on his errand.

Back at a very crowded flat, Keira calls the Red Sock Ninjas outside for a quick briefing.

"I've got an idea, but it might put us back in danger of being found. Is that a problem?"

Well of course it's a problem but we need to hear the plan first.

It's a rubbish plan but what other options have we got?

Jack turns up with the phone which Keira hands to Naz.

She then calls her Mum Joan and explains what's going on before handing the phone to Keira.

"Joan, I know you theatre people always talk about how the show must go on. Any chance you can call Miss Rainey and remind her? For old times sake?"

I'd forgotten that Joan used to work with Miss Rainey way back.

Now all we can do is wait.

I hate waiting. We're all just standing there getting fidgety when the mobile goes off and makes us all jump.

"Hello?"

While Keira's talking to Joan, Miss G flies out of the flat waving her mobile.

"I've just had Miss Rainey back on. She says we can use the school!"

I quickly hide behind Red in case Miss wants to hug me again.

"She's going to meet us there in ten minutes."

Keira tells Miss to get everyone over to the school and only I notice her taking the battery and SIM card out of the phone before handing it all to Jack.

"Give it a good wipe and dump it would you please?"

I think she wants her fingerprints to disappear from the buttons. Phoning Joan could be dangerous if our enemies are monitoring the calls. They might trace the mobile to this town and come looking for us. That's why it's never going to make another call and will probably end up in several different rubbish bins or sunk in the river.

The next half hour goes very quickly as we get everyone into the school.

"Tammy, show everyone into our classroom and get them changed. Rehearsal's in ten minutes!"

"Anyone with a mobile, phone home and tell everyone to come here for the show tonight and not to the hut. Tell them to spread the news."

"Jamie, check out the desks and see if everything's still connected."

If it isn't then we've got a problem.

"I'll help him," shouts Naz.

What she really means is that I'll be helping her.

Do you know what happens when schools close for the holidays?

That's when floors get washed, polished and generally deep cleaned which I suppose is why the Hall's nearly empty with all the chairs and stuff pushed to the edges.

We find the lighting and sound desks carefully stacked in a corner but without a trace of wiring. So where's the cables all hiding then?

"Start at the other end," says Naz logically. "Cleaners don't tend to de-rig lamps."

We follow the wiring from the lights to the cable and down the wall where it disappears into a forest of chair legs. I crawl as close as I can get and lift the cable until Naz can loop it over the top of the chairs. We then move along a bit and do the same again until eventually we find the rest of the cable coiled behind another stack of chairs.

"That'll need taping down," says a voice and I turn to find Miss Rainey stood there in a pair of jeans and trainers.

"I'll go find some gaffer tape while you two lay out the cable."

In case you don't know, gaffer tape is a very wide, black, strong sticky tape and it holds everything in the theatre together according to Naz. It sticks cables to floors, scenery to walls, and can even hold costumes together in a rush.

And everything's now in a rush.

Peter Marney

Tick tock

Jack and Tufty have ignored their own advice and gone back to salvage the scenery which they're now trying to fit onto our school stage. This is at the same time as the dancers are practising on the stage and changing stuff so they don't fall off the front or sides.

Lucky for us, the lighting desk still has all the lamps labelled so it's just a case of finding the right wire to attach to the correct labelled input. What really happens is Naz sticks a wire in a socket and I shout out which light comes on. She then moves the wire to the correct label and then we start again with the next wire.

Miss Rainey leaves several rolls of tape and goes off to join Miss G and find someone else to help.

"I'd forgotten what theatre's supposed to be about," she says. "I'm so glad Joan reminded me."

I'd have loved to hear that conversation!

Half an hour later and we've got a lighting desk. Naz has also made it simpler and shows me what she's done.

"This slider controls all of these lamps," she says, moving it so I can see what happens.

"The first four sliders all work on groups just like that one."

All good so far.

"Side lamps here and here for each side of the stage."

That looks good.

"The rest are all singles so just have a play and see what happens while I track down the speaker wiring for the music."

I can smell fish and chips and pizza!

As I'm stuffing my mouth with food I find out that Miss Rainey's been onto the local radio station and told them all about what's happened. People listening to the show have just been turning up to help or to bring food and drink.

Sparky, an electrician who arrived out of nowhere, double checks our wiring and sorts out the sound while a couple of Mums are busy with sewing machines fixing costumes. Everyone is talking about how the town needs more of these community events and the place is buzzing with activity.

The stage is too busy for me to play with lights so I wander about a bit and make myself useful.

In one of the breaks I find out why Amy was late this morning.

"Uncle say two men come asking questions."

Someone's found out about them and is sniffing around for more information. Uncle says it's dangerous to stay so, after the show, they're being taken to another town and another hiding place.

Why are they being treated like criminals?

All of this news makes me jumpy. If our phone call gets traced then we'll also have some men looking for us and could end up just the same as Amy and Malik. Keira's already warned us to watch out for anything strange and insisted we pack an emergency bag each in case we have to leave quickly.

Sometimes, being a Red Sock Ninja isn't fun at all.

But other times, like right at this minute, it can be really exciting.

Right at this minute I'm jumping at full speed over someone's back fence, into their garden, and out again the other side on my way to a small park I've just found.

It's Keira's idea and she's given each of us a different direction to explore. We're to find a few escape routes from school just in case we need to disappear quickly. It makes sense to be prepared and she's also given us a secret place to meet up again should we need to run in separate directions.

Of course it does mean that we miss our break but the exercise does us good and we're just back in time to start another run through of the show but this time in full costume.

I'm still undecided about the lighting but come up with some good effects which seem to fit what's happening on stage. Maybe this show's going to work after all.

Half way through I notice two figure sneak into the darkened hall and sit at the back. They're quickly joined by what looks like Miss Rainey and they seem to be chatting.

This doesn't look good.

But when I bring the lights up at the end of the show I get a surprise. Not as big a surprise as Naz but it's still nice to see her Mums. Both the Red Sock girls fly off of the stage and into the arms of Paula and Joan for long hugs which I get included in as soon as I join them.

Later I hear Paula whisper to Keira about changing trains three times and leaving their mobiles at home. They've been using some of our tricks in case anyone tried to follow them.

It seems that Miss Rainey invited them up to see the show and it would look too suspicious if they refused. Besides, Joan wanted to join in the fun of helping with a show again.

"Come on Jay," she says, remembering to use my new name, "let's have a look at this desk of yours."

According to Naz, her Mum used to be a lighting wiz and did it as a proper job with real actors and big theatres. I explain that Naz helped me with the wiring and she smiles.

"I taught her that trick of grouping lamps together," she says. "Nice set up, you're doing a good job."

Actually it was a bit rubbish but she can see I'm working without cues and making it up as we go along.

It's about now that things get really busy.

We're all given ten minutes to go outside for some fresh air before preparing for the show. Everyone else starts getting the hall ready and the chairs laid out for the audience. Someone's been listening to the local radio station and they've been reminding people about our show tonight and telling them to come and support us.

On my way out I sneak a peek around the front of the school and see a long line of people waiting to get in.

I also notice something else that really shouldn't be there.

Plan A

Keira's sent Jack for a wander and he's spotted the same as me.

"Black car, tinted windows and a funny aerial sticking up. Looks like two people inside but I can't be sure."

There's more.

"I went a bit further and, tucked up a side street, there's a big van. Bit like a builders truck but not one I recognise and I know most of the guys round here. And guess what? It's got the same aerial sticking up out of the roof."

They must have traced the phone call.

We nearly got kidnapped in one of those vans. This isn't looking good and it's probably time for Plan A where we run away before they spring their trap but it just doesn't feel right.

"If we're not here, what happens to the show? Miss will have to give the people their money back and then it's all been for nothing."

Joan could run the desk but she's only seen half the show and anyway, they'll have to run away as well just in case.

Keira's all for going right now but Red and Naz agree with me and say they're staying until the end of the show. As soon as it's over, we run, and we run fast.

Keira sends Jack back to the flat, if it's not being watched, to grab our bags and they agree to meet behind the library where he'll have a car waiting for us. The Red Sock Ninjas then put their heads together and share the escape routes we've found. I also notice Jack handing Keira another new mobile so they can stay in touch during the escape.

I've got the most difficult exit as I'm stuck in the middle of the hall with the desks. We agree that Joan will sit with me and get in the way if anyone tries to chase me. Once I'm backstage then it's easy to get out of the building and away.

Luckily, Miss is too busy to notice all of this going on which is just as well because we're about to add to her last minute troubles.

Naz has suddenly started a migraine which is a sort of really bad headache which can make you feel sick and dizzy. She hasn't

really, but we need an excuse so
she doesn't have to be on stage
dancing. Red's job is already only
in the wings helping dancers and it
makes sense if Naz does the same if
a quick escape is needed during the
show.

Miss isn't happy and Naz agrees to
get ready and just sit backstage in
case she feels well enough to
dance.

Then the doors open and people
flood in to fill the seats in the
hall. As I come in to take my seat
by the lighting desk I notice that
there's even people standing at the
back of the hall. Every seat is
taken.

Like everyone working backstage,
I'm dressed in black so as not to
stand out. That's what always
happens and tonight it might be
doubly useful, especially with my
ninja hood tucked in my pocket. I
know the girls are dressed the same

even if Naz has had to put a
costume over the top of her blacks.

 I dim the lights and the show
starts.

 As we're back in school I've now
got a headset and can hear what's
happening backstage. Miss is
sitting at the piano but she's
managing to whisper comments
between the singing. It all seems
to be going quite well.

 Everyone on stage is smiling and
the singing is better than I've
heard it during the whole weekend.
I'm actually beginning to enjoy
myself even if I am super busy and
really focussed on fitting the
lighting to the show.

 Suddenly we get to the interval
where everyone gets a break for
twenty minutes to go for a wee or
whatever. That's when I notice
we're not the only people with
headsets.

 There's a man and a woman having a
whispered conversation at the back

of the hall. The thing is, they're on opposite sides of the hall and seem to be talking to themselves if you're not really looking out for these things.

They're just standing there at the moment so I guess they won't want to do anything until the end of the show. Just to make sure, I dim the house lights well before the twenty minutes are up which sort of forces everyone quickly back to their seats.

Keira's been helping Malik and Tufty change the sets on stage but I can hear her on the headset telling everyone that, as there's nothing to do for the next ten minutes, she's going outside for a cigarette.

Strange time to take up smoking, especially when you keep telling us what a filthy habit it is.

Guess who's going for a quiet wander?

Wish I had a spare ten minutes. I know it looks easy when you're in the audience but lighting can be quite tricky. It's not just turn off some lights at the start and put them back on at the end. Anyway, that's why I don't have time to notice too much other than my desk for the next twenty minutes.

Then I hear Keira's voice on the headset again.

"Anyone seen my torch?"

That's a code word we agreed earlier. It means "Amber Alert". I think she's found something on her wander.

Amber isn't Red but it isn't Green either. It's a sort of get ready to move colour, a bit like traffic lights. I ease my chair back a bit and make sure I can see a clear passage to the side of the hall where I can then slide backstage.

"Jay," Keira whispers again, "can you hand over to Joan and get back here? Nothing serious but we need some more light backstage left. One of the bulbs has blown."

 This isn't code and I don't know what's going on.

 I do now.

Plan B

Backstage left I find the rest of the Red Sock Ninjas.

"We need a new plan," says Keira.

I liked Plan A. It was a nice simple plan and didn't involve me being chased by two policemen. It's alright for Red and Keira, they get the easy way out. It's me and Naz who are the one's being chased and she's not as fast as me.

They came at us straight after the end of the show and we barely had time to make a run for it. We might have had a better chance if someone hadn't shouted "They went that way" so the men could follow us.

I'm gasping for breathe and trying not to slip in the wet. Despite our head start, the two men are getting closer. Naz is definitely slowing down and if we don't come up with something soon, she's going to be captured.

I'm wondering how to help when I hear her fall over.

"Keep running!" she shouts from the ground. "Go!"

For once I do as I'm told and speed up to leave her behind. I'm back over the same fence as earlier and through the small park and out the other side. From there I can slip into the alleyways behind the houses and then back to the flat where I hope to meet up with what's left of the Red Sock Ninja Clan.

Naz has been captured. There's no way she'll have been able to fall like that and still escape.

Of course I'm right but I don't find out the whole story until later.

The two men drag Naz back to the school and straight into Paula and Joan who start firing questions at them.

"Why are you chasing our daughter?"

"Is she being arrested?"

"What for?"

The policemen look puzzled.

"Daughter?"

He probably couldn't get his head around the idea of someone having two Mums.

Paula then tells Naz to take off her costume which she swears she was only wearing for the show.

"Costume?"

It's about now that the men realise they've been chasing the wrong girl. I guess it's an easy mistake to make. After all, these small dark girls all look the same in that headscarf thing don't they?

Well, that was what we hoped when we came up with the plan.

It started with Keira's wander.

"I went for a walk by that van and stopped to light a cigarette so I could get a good look."

I was sure she didn't smoke.

"Anyway, the door slides open and this policeman gets out and asks me for a light. But he's not a proper copper. They have these numbers on their shoulders but his just says Border Force."

So?

"They're here for Ami and Malik. They're immigration police."

That's why we came up with Plan B.

Ami and Malik will run away as soon as they start being chased while the Red Socks create a diversion.

Actually, me with Naz wearing Ami's hijab will run away and hope that we look enough like Malik and Amy that we'll get chased.

Red's shouting helped persuade the men to follow us.

In the meantime our two Iraqis were smuggled out through the bushes and into a waiting car where Jack drove them away.

Naz says that when she saw two angry men running towards her, she just followed when Malik told her to run. Paula explains that her daughter's had trouble in the past due to her colour and was understandably scared of strange men trying to chase her.

This last point is also made to another young lady who's standing nearby and holding a notepad. What with all the fuss on the radio, the local paper has sent a reporter down to cover the show and she's got more of a story than she expected.

"So, do you just chase small dark skinned girls or must they be wearing a hijab?" she asks. "Should I start running?"

She's small and dark too and making the two policemen very uncomfortable.

"I'm afraid Miss," says one of them, "that we can't comment on operational matters."

About now they decide they're needed elsewhere and leave, although the reporter follows them to the door still asking questions. While she's distracted, Naz and her Mums sneak out of another door to avoid any pending photographs.

Keira's also managed to have a word with Miss G so that by the time the reporter does come back nobody really knows anything about anyone. Everyone's delighted that

Ami and Malik have escaped and nobody wants to get Naz or me into trouble.

Keira even manages to persuade Miss to look after Dog Girl until the morning just in case reporters come round to the flat. It's not much of an excuse but Miss is so pleased that the project went well that she's not thinking straight and would probably agree to anything.

It's a shame that we couldn't help clear up after the show but we did have a little party with Naz's Mums and told them all about school and stuff. Red even got to send messages back home to her family which Joan promised to deliver together with a photo Keira took on her phone and printed out.

Of course it all ended in tears when they had to leave for home but it was nice to see them even if it was only for a short while.

The next edition of the local paper has a picture of our stage on the front page and a story about the show inside.

According to Naz, who is doing the reading, the front page story's about heavy handed tactics by police against immigrants trying to join in with the local community. They've even got a quote from a local politician saying that the show project is just what the area needs to involve all local children no matter where they come from. Maybe Miss can ask him for some money next year.

Naz has decided that she's never going to wear a hijab again and she's also had her hair cut really short. It looks good and more importantly makes her look completely different.

We're all keeping an eye out just in case we get any more unwanted attention and we're keeping our

emergency bags packed and ready
just in case.

Talking of unwanted attention,
Red's just given me some more bad
news.

"Dog Girl's just told me that she
thinks you're really cute."

Oh my!

The End

Peter Marney

The next book in the series

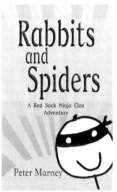

 Has Red set up Jamie on a date with Dog Girl? If so, why is he now running around in circles? Maybe it's got something to do with the fact that the enemy have at last found them again.

 The Red Sock Ninjas must use all of their skills in this last adventure if they are to escape and live happily ever after.

Peter Marney

About the author

Peter Marney lives by the sea, is just as bad at drawing as Jamie, and falls over if his socks don't have the right day of the week written on them.

On a more serious note, Peter has worked supporting children with reading difficulties and understands some of their problems. He is passionate about the importance of both reading and storytelling to the growing mind.

Peter Marney

The Red Sock Ninja Clan Adventures

Birth of a Ninja

Jamie's about to start another new school and has been told to stay out of trouble. Like that's going to happen!

It's not as if he wants to fight but you've got to help out if a girl's being picked on, right? Even if it does turn out that she's the best fighter in the school and laughs at your odd socks.

Follow Jamie as he makes friends, sorts out a big problem at his school, and discovers that his weird new babysitter knows secret ninja skills.

Hide and Seek

Find out why Jamie hates dogs and why he's hiding in a school cupboard in the dark. Has it got something to do with Keira's new training games for the Red Sock Ninjas?

The Mystery Intruder

Someone is playing in school after dark and it's not just the Red Sock Ninjas. Maybe Harry knows who it is but he's not talking so Jamie will have to find another way to solve this mystery.

The Mighty Porcupine

What do you do when your enemy is too powerful to fight? Has somebody finally beaten the Red Sock Ninjas?

The Mystery Troublemakers

Someone wants to get Jamie's new youth club into trouble but why?

Maybe the Red Sock Ninjas can find the answer by climbing rooftops or will it just get them into more trouble?

Statty Sticks

Why is Jamie being attacked by a small girl who isn't Red and why does he get the feeling that someone is spying on him?

Has it got anything to do with why his school is in danger and how numbers can lie?

Enemies and Friends

Why has Jamie got a new uncle and why does everyone end up hiding in bushes?

Have the Red Sock Ninjas now found too big a porcupine and will it spell disaster for their future together?

Run Away Success

Where do you run to when everything goes wrong? That's the latest problem for the Red Sock Ninjas and this time Wally isn't around to mastermind the plan.

With the enemy closing in for capture, the friends must split up and disappear. Is this the end of the Clan or the beginning of a whole new experience for Jamie?

Rise and Shine

Why does going to the library get Jamie into a fight and what's that got to do with Keira's plan for getting rid of him?

Helping to put on a show with Miss G was difficult enough without guess who turning up. Yet again the Red Socks must use their skills to save the day and the show.

Rabbits and Spiders

Has Red set up Jamie on a date with Dog Girl? If so, why is he now running around in circles? Maybe it's got something to do with the fact that the enemy have at last found them again.

The Red Sock Ninjas must use all of their skills in this last adventure if they are to escape and live happily ever after.

Printed in Great Britain
by Amazon